D0811214

SONS AND DAUGHTERS

J. C. de Graft

SONS

and

DAUGHTERS

LONDON
Oxford University Press
ACCRA
1964

Oxford University Press, Amen House, London E.C.4

GLASGOW NEW YORK TORONTO MELBOURNE WELLINGTON
BOMBAY CALCUTTA MADRAS KARACHI LAHORE DACCA
CAPE TOWN SALISBURY NAIROBI IBADAN ACCRA
KUALA LUMPUR HONG KONG

This play is fully protected by copyright and all
applications for public performance should be made to
Oxford University Press,
Amen House, Warwick Square, London, E.C.4

PRINTED IN ENGLAND BY
HAZELL WATSON AND VINEY LTD
AYLESBURY, BUCKS

822. 91.

Characters
(in order of appearance)

AARON OFOSU
AWERE, his friend
HANNAH, Aaron's mother
ADWOA, a maidservant
MAANAN, sister to Aaron
FOSUWA, paternal aunt to Aaron
  and Maanan

LAWYER BONU, a friend of the
  Ofosu family
JAMES OFOSU, father
GEORGE, brother to Aaron and
  Maanan
MRS. BONU, wife to Lawyer
  Bonu

The scene is the sitting-room of the Ofosus' house

If the producer should think it necessary to have
an interval, it should occur between the first and
second acts. Strictly, the author would prefer
that the play went on without an interval.

ACT ONE

The sitting-room of the Ofosus' house. The style of furnishing is rather typical of the urban household. There is a leaning to the obviously imported or European. The only item of traditional furniture is a large mahogany elephant stool. Other items: wooden arm-chairs with puffed cushions; a low central round table fitted with 'coffee' tables that can be pulled out as needed; a metal trolley with an impressive array of expensive drinks—and cheap glasses; a large radiogram; a few photographs in black and white. The most conspicuous item of furniture is a very large, coloured wall calendar advertising heavy-duty truck tyres.

There are three curtained doors. One (R) leads into the dining room; another (UC) takes one to the bedrooms upstairs; the third (L) to the street.

The scene opens to a lot of background noise—familiar compound noises: women talking as they go about their household work, a crying child being loudly upbraided by the mother, etc.

Aaron Ofosu and Awere are revealed. Awere is sitting down, in thought, holding a folded newspaper; and Aaron is standing, speaking to Awere. On the round table, in front of Awere, is a box of oil colours.

AARON: So there we are, Awere. I don't know what to do now. It seems I have to give up all my plans.

AWERE: Is it as bad as that? I still think you can do something about it, you know. Persuade him; make him see how frustrating the whole business is bound to be for you. Surely, he ought to know that one can take a horse to the water, but one cannot force it to drink!

AARON: He knows that all right; but he will tell you I am not a horse and engineering is anything but water. He expects me to appreciate the sacrifice he is making giving me a professional education. But really it is not a sacrifice at all: he has plenty of dough, if it comes to that; but he likes to think of it as a sacrifice, and there's nothing I can say to that. And then there is the prestige to the family, to say nothing of his long cherished hope that all his children will become professional men—and women.

AWERE: What do you mean 'professional women'?

AARON: I mean precisely that .

AWERE: He doesn't want Maanan to do mechanical engineering too, does he?

AARON: Man, you make me laugh! My eldest brother, George, is a doctor, don't forget; and we are expecting Kofi back next September—a fully qualified chartered accountant. You want to hear the old man telling his friends of his son who is a 'medical man', and the great things he expects of his other son who is going to be a banker!

AWERE: Yes; but what does he want Maanan to do?

AARON: Hasn't Maanan told you?

AWERE: I know she wants to make dancing a career.

AARON: And Father wants her to become a lawyer, Ghana's first lady lawyer, as he puts it!

AWERE: But there are several women lawyers about already....

AARON: I know; but does Father care about that?

AWERE: Is that why he got her that job with Lawyer Bonu?

AARON: Yes; and that's why Maanan is unhappy. [*A pause.*]

AWERE: What is she going to do about it?

AARON: I don't know. The whole thing has become so painfully unbearable that I am not surprised Maanan has never told you. But I know Maanan can be tough. The old man does not know that; and he is no doubt thinking that because Maanan hasn't kicked up any fuss so far, all is well and will continue to be well. In fact, I overheard him asking Lawyer Bonu to hasten up his inquiries about a place in a

law school in UK for Maanan. Maanan simply smiled when
I told her about it.

AWERE: Does your brother George know about all this?

AARON: All this what?

AWERE: Maanan's unwillingness to become a lawyer and your
father's determination that she will become one.

AARON: I expect he does.

AWERE: And what does he say?

AARON: [*sceptically.*] What do you expect George to say?

AWERE: At least, advise your father against forcing Maanan.

AARON: Will Father admit that he is forcing Maanan?

AWERE: Oh, I see.

AARON: I'm glad you do.

[*Aaron's mother, Hannah, who has been in the kitchen during
this conversation, now appears at the door (R). She is a woman of
about forty-five, quiet and dignified in bearing, and wears
cloth and sandals. She is clearly illiterate, but she has been well
brought up, and this impression of her is enhanced by her good
looks. She is holding a porcelain dish and a napkin with
which she has obviously been wiping the dish.*]

HANNAH: Aaron.

AARON: Yes, Mother.

HANNAH: Oh, Awere is still here; I thought he had left. [*Awere
stands up, smiling easily like one who knows that he is
accepted by a good friend's mother.*] No, Awere, sit down. I
only wanted to know what time it is. Aaron, what's the
time?

AARON: [*looking at his wrist watch.*] Just about five o'clock,
Mother.

HANNAH: I'm sure your father will be home soon. Have you
been for the mail?

AARON: No, Mother, Maanan said she would collect them on
her way home past the Post Office.

HANNAH: All right. [*Exit.*]

AWERE: Well, Aaron, if your old man is due home soon, then I
must be shifting. I have an idea that he thinks I am
responsible for your wanting to paint instead of
obediently falling in with his plans. And [*he taps the folded
newspaper he has been holding all this time*] now that
everybody knows of this scholarship and the success of my
exhibition, he will say—and I think quite justifiably—that
I have come here to put more ideas into your head.
[*Awere takes up the box of oil colours. Aaron looks
disconsolately at his friend, then sits down on the arm of a chair
and sighs.*]

AARON: [*like one who has been paying no attention.*] What galls
me is wasting my time and talents like this! Two whole
years of Sixth Form, studying history and economics and
Latin and heaven only knows what else, when I could have
been painting and sculpting—developing and realizing
myself . . . But I may yet make it, and follow you to
London. All I need really is a place in an Art School, and
engineering can go hang itself.

AWERE: [*slowly reading Aaron's meaning.*] You mean you will
make your father send you over in the belief that you're
going to do engineering, then switch over to art whilst in
London?

AARON: Precisely that!

AWERE: But that's the craziest thing you could do.

AARON: How so?

AWERE: Do you know what I would do if a son of mine took
me for a ride like that?

AARON: There's nothing you could do.

AWERE: Plenty.

AARON: Like . . . ?

AWERE: Like cutting your allowance. I hear there's nothing
worse than getting stranded in London whilst studying.

AARON: I could work, couldn't I?

AWERE: And I wouldn't stop at cutting your allowance if I
seriously took exception to your becoming a painter.

AARON: What more would you do?

AWERE: Request the Ghana Office in London to pack you back
home! [*A pause.*]

AARON: You wouldn't do that, surely . . .

AWERE: Your father might, if I know him well enough. No,
my dear fellow, you'd be cutting your own throat if you
attempted to deceive your old man like that. The best
thing is to try to persuade him to see differently. For
example . . .

[*Enter a young maidservant (R) holding a steaming pan of slops.
She is obliviously crossing the room towards the L, when Aaron
suddenly shouts at her.*]

AARON: Hey! Go back!

MAIDSERVANT: Ewuraba asked me to go and empty it into
the drain outside.

AARON: [*his temper rising.*] Did she tell you to go out through
this room?

MAIDSERVANT: But she said . . .

AARON: She didn't say anything! If I catch you going through
here again with slops, you'll see what I'll do. Isn't there
another way out of the kitchen? [*The maidservant turns
back into the kitchen reluctantly.*] This sort of thing drives
me mad! If the Cabinet itself were in session here that
girl would walk right through with that thing. And yet
Mother is at her all day trying to polish her up . . . My God!

AWERE: Why do you allow every little thing to upset you like
this? Anyway as I was going to say, if you could persuade
your father to see that art also pays—or could pay—he
might be induced to give in, even respect your choice of
occupation.

AARON: That's an idea. But painting and money—well, I
simply hate the idea. I want to paint because I like to

paint; I want to express myself in paint, I want to create
works of art, things of beauty.

AWERE : [*suddenly bursting out laughing.*] I don't care for such
clichés, Aaron. Things of beauty indeed ! Whom are you
trying to convince—me or yourself?

AARON : [*suddenly freezing with intense emotion.*] You are lucky.
Nobody tries to bully you out of your choice. Your father
is proud of your talent. I don't know of your mother,
but . . .

AWERE : Your mother is not against you too?

AARON : She's all right. [*A pause, as if undecided what to say. Then,
with a shrug of the shoulders.*] But what can she do to help
me? [*More quietly.*] Good simple soul, she is as much a
victim as myself, only she does not know . . . [*A pause.*] No
doubt you think it improper for me to talk like this—
well . . . [*Another shrug of the shoulders.*]

AWERE : Come, come: I think you are making a mountain out
of an anthill.

AARON: [*flaring up.*] I'm not ! I said you are lucky, but you
don't know how lucky. To you painting is simply a
matter of getting to work with brush and paint and doing
what you like with your time. Your failures are your
incentive, your spur. Here in this house things are
different. Even my successes are held up against me. The
old man is jealous of my very materials. You'd like to see
him eyeing my sketch-book. [*He suddenly dashes out* (C) *and
returns with a torn canvas—an unfinished painting.*] Do you see
this? The old man tore it—he tore right through it. But
I've never told you of this. He threw my easel out of the
window, because he stumbled on it in the corridor. As for
turpentine, he simply hates the smell of it. Drives him
stark mad. [*Another pause.*] Yes, here things are different. I
must keep convincing myself that painting is worthwhile,
that art is a great calling; I must keep hammering it into

my heart that beauty does matter: the powers against me
in this house are greater than you imagine. [*Another pause.
Awere is looking intently at Aaron.*] Even these walls are
against me. Look; look around you: look at that awful
print on the wall there; look at these cushion covers . . .
[*More quietly.*] Do you now understand me? Do you, now?
Everything in this room outrages my sense of beauty,
undermines my will to create pictures of lasting appeal, and
I must keep fighting back or I'm lost.

AWERE: I see what you mean; only, I feel slightly uneasy when
you talk so passionately of beauty. . . . Does Maanan feel
the same as you?

AARON: I don't know. But I'll tell you a story. Once upon a
time Maanan took it into her head to freshen up this room
with flowers, real flowers: nothing much, but real flowers
and leaves with sap in them. I don't know what came over
her, but she returned home one evening with a bunch of
frangipani, sweet and white. She set them on that table
there. What did the old man say when he saw those
frangipani? 'Rubbish!' Next morning he emptied them
himself into the dust pan. My heart ached. Maanan said
never a word; but she never made another such mistake.
Now look what we have: a permanent bloom of ugly
paper flowers! [*Awere laughs.*] Is it so funny? I felt like
slaying the man who made them. I was alone in here when
he brought them in. 'Whose are they?' I asked him. 'Your
father ordered them. They're the best bunch I ever made.
Don't you like them?' I told him to go hang with his
flowers.

AWERE: You did?

AARON: Yes, and Father nearly disowned me when he came
home that day. After leaving these flowers here that rat
had gone to the office and told him I said I didn't like
them. Father wanted to know how I dared to question

his taste. Didn't I know he had paid thirty shillings for them? [*Silence.*] Anything that money can buy: that's it. Or anything that can bring in money! [*Quietly but intensely.*] But one day I'm going to tell everybody to go hang with their money.

AWERE: Are you sure you aren't being too idealistic?

AARON: That's the trouble with the old man, with this country of ours, with everybody. Art must bring in money, or there will be no art—no painting, no writing, no drama, no dancing, no music. Our society is sold on money: nothing is worth anything unless it brings in money; and those who have the talent to be real great artists—what do they do about it? They allow our philistine public to browbeat them into submission, they dare not love their calling, they dare not give themselves heart and soul to her, they are ashamed of her because she wears no golden ornaments.

AWERE: Fine talk again. Don't forget that I also want to paint; but even if a man were a genius, he'd have to buy himself some materials ...

AARON: But I'm damned if I'm going to treat painting merely as a source of income; what's more, I'd rather kill myself than make the old man think that I have chosen to paint simply because of the money it will bring me.

AWERE: Money also is important, you know; you cannot do without it.

AARON: You hit the nail on the head all right, Awere. My father talks of family prestige; he talks of giving his children the best education; he talks of the dignity of the professions; but all the time he has his eye only on the money. What does he care about medicine, the joy of healing, the satisfaction—the hard-earned satisfaction— of bringing broken bodies back to life from the very jaws of death? What does he care? What does anybody care?

AWERE: Now you're talking as if you were in love with surgery too.

AARON: I don't love surgery and that's why I don't care to become a surgeon—or a lawyer, for that matter. But my brother George cares for surgery, he loves it. O.K. he goes ahead. He goes ahead and does it. Why not? But he was lucky because the old man happened to like the profession he chose for himself. I think Kofi also loves his ledgers, and he too was lucky that Father liked his choice. But I have the curse on me: the curse of the non-conformist. The old man thinks that George and Kofi are obedient sons; he actually believes that he chose their professions for them; while I, his last son, and Maanan, a mere slip of a girl—we, the two youngest of his children, who must just fit in with his plans and obey his every command—we dare to find fault with his choice, we disobey him! [*Enter Maanan.* L. *She is a girl of eighteen, and very pretty. She wears cloth and is holding a newspaper. On one arm hangs an office handbag of strong leather, and she carries the air of a girl coming home from work. But Maanan does not look cheerful, and one would expect her to throw her things down on a table and flop into a chair. She does neither of these things, however. When she sees Aaron and Awere—who have both turned to look in her direction—she gives a wan smile and walks into the room, adjusting the 'ahatar' hanging from her shoulder. Aaron, caught at the end of his passionate speech, is looking embarrassed; Awere does not stand up, but he returns Maanan's smile.*]

AWERE: Hullo, Maanan; you don't look cheerful this afternoon.

MAANAN: Hullo, you two.

AARON: What's the matter, Maanan? Have you lost a boy friend?

MAANAN: Don't let Father hear you saying that. [*Going to the table and putting down her newspaper.*] Is he home yet, by the way?

AARON: No, he isn't.

AWERE: I shouldn't be here with you if he were. [*Getting up.*] Well, folks, I must be pushing off now. [*Moves towards door L, and nearly collides with Aunt as she enters.*]

AWERE: [*springing aside.*] Sorry!

AUNT: [*walks past Awere, looking straight at Aaron and Maanan.*] I thought so! [*An ominous pause.*] Where's your mother?

AARON: She's in the kitchen.

[*Aunt now looks menacingly at Awere, then exit (R) into the kitchen.*]

AWERE: That's the warning light, I'm afraid. I must be off before your aunt returns.

AARON: Wait a minute, I'll come with you. [*To Maanan.*] What's the matter with you, Maanan?

MAANAN: Oh, nothing. Just fed up with life.

AARON: By the way, did you collect the mail? I told Mother you said you'd collect it yourself on your way back home.

MAANAN: [*like one who suddenly remembers.*] O God! I forgot . . .

AARON: That's all right. I can collect it myself. Awere will come with me, eh, Awere? We shall return before Father comes home. Then I shall take you along to the Arts Centre to close down your exhibition for the day. O.K.? Give me the box key, Maanan.

MAANAN: Oh, I'm very sorry, Awere. [*Fumbling in her handbag for the key.*] I should have congratulated you on your exhibition. The papers were full of praise this morning. In fact I brought this copy of the *Daily Clarion* home so I could read all the fine things they're saying about your work. . . .

AWERE: Thanks, Maanan. I was terribly upset when I didn't

see you at the opening yesterday. I looked everywhere for
you.

MAANAN: I tried to come.

AWERE: Yes, I know. But I couldn't believe it when Aaron
told me he feared that awful lawyer employer of yours
had kept you in again with work. Anyway, now you've
congratulated me, I forgive you.

MAANAN: And your scholarship to Goldsmith College—you're
lucky, aren't you? I wish I also could do just the things
I'd like most to do.

AWERE: Nothing prevents you.

MAANAN: Don't tease me, Awere. You know very well …
Anyway, I need not bother you with my headaches.
Here's the key, Aaron. I'll be going to see the exhibition
tomorrow, Awere, come what may; and I hope I'll see
you again soon, to tell you what I think of it.

AWERE: I'll look forward to that.

AARON: [*who has taken the key from Maanan.*] Come on, fellow,
let's get going. I don't like Father to come home and find
that the mail has not been collected. [*Just before he and
Awere vanish through the door* L.] And, by the way, tell
Mother I've gone to collect the mail, will you?

AWERE: What about this box of pigments? Couldn't I leave it
here meantime?

AARON: Of course! [*Awere returns to set the box of colours down
on the table, but keeps the newspaper. Then exit with
Aaron* L. *Maanan, left alone, stands for a while lost in
thought; then she sighs. A moment later, re-enter Aunt
followed by an anxious Hannah.*]

AUNT: He's gone. [*To Maanan.*] Where's that boy?

MAANAN: Aaron? He's gone to collect the letters.

AUNT: I mean that boy who keeps coming here to see you.

MAANAN: Awere? Awere does not come here to see me.

AUNT: Don't pretend. I saw you with my own eyes today.

MAANAN: I am not pretending ...

AUNT: [*turning on Hannah.*] I must tell James about this when he comes home. I think he must do something about it.

HANNAH: What are you going to tell James? What has Maanan done?

AUNT: If you kept your eyes open you would know. But I will not sit by with my hands between my legs while my brother's daughter is ruined.

MAANAN: But what have I done?

HANNAH: Leave us alone, Maanan. [*Exit Maanan UC, rather reluctantly.*] Now, Fosuwa, your brother is my husband; but that is no reason why you should take it upon yourself to run my affairs for me. This sort of thing has gone on for too long, and I must tell you now that I don't want any more interference from you either in my affairs or in my children's.

AUNT: Interference! [*Getting quarrelsome.*] Is it interference to want my niece properly married? Tell me—is it?

HANNAH: I have said all I have to say.

AUNT: I haven't yet! And whose house do you think this is? I ask you—whose? So long as I remain in this house ...

HANNAH: You mean so long as I remain in this house! I knew you would come round to that sooner or later: you always have. But I am not here because I like being here; I wouldn't be if I had my own way. But James will like to stay on here in his family house, and so for seven years now—ever since we returned home from Sekondi—I have had to put up with the whole lot of you and your ceaseless interference. Don't you ever consider that I too have people?

AUNT: Why don't you go to them? Who is forcing you to stay on with James?

HANNAH: You will not understand, Fosuwa—you never will; but when a woman has lived with her husband for as long

as I have with James, and has had children with him as old
as mine, and has helped him to build up all he has from
nothing—a woman who has done all this does not get up
any day and leave her husband the way you suggest—even
if that husband has relatives like you. [*Exit door* UC.]

AUNT: [*shouting after Hannah.*] Helped him to build up from
nothing! And what were you yourself when James
married you? Eh, tell me—what were you? Tchweaa!
[*Turning to leave the room.*] But James is to blame—not you.
[*Enter Lawyer B* (L), *preceded by the maidservant dangling her
pan, now empty. Lawyer B is about forty, clean shaven but
for a neat moustache, and wears a very neat and expensive-
looking dark suit. His coming paunch and full cheeks mark him
as a prosperous man, and his very white semi-stiff collar, dark
tie and suit emphasize this impression. Without being told so,
one can readily guess that he is a lawyer. He pauses, then
advances, his face lit up by a broad smile. He is effusive in his
manner.*]

LAWYER B: Good evening. [*Shaking Aunt's hand.*] How are
you?

AUNT: [*suddenly changed and all charm.*] Good evening, Lawyer.
I am very well. Oh, won't you sit down? I'm sure you
want to see Maanan—I'll send for her. [*Turning to
maidservant.*] Hey, Adwoa, go and tell Maanan that
Lawyer is here. She is upstairs. Tell her to be quick.
[*Exit maidservant, first into kitchen* R *to put down her pan, and
then back and out again* UC.]

LAWYER B: [*sitting down.*] Thank you. I was passing by and I
thought I might drop in to see James and Hannah. Are
they in?

AUNT: [*also sitting down.*] No, James is not back yet from work.

LAWYER B: How is he?

AUNT: Oh, he is well. [*A pause.*]

LAWYER B: [*looking at watch.*] Actually, I did not intend to

stay long, and especially as James is not in yet, I'd rather
drop in again later this evening. I have an appointment . . .

AUNT: But you'd like to see Maanan, wouldn't you? [*Getting
up and going to door.*] Maanan, Maanan, Lawyer is here.
Will you come down—he is in a hurry? [*Comes back to
chair, looking very satisfied.*]

LAWYER B: [*unconvincingly.*] I wonder . . . she must be tired,
don't you think? I am afraid I have been overworking
her at the office lately. So many cases these days that
there's hardly any rest for any of us. But Maanan
works hard.

AUNT: I'm glad you like Maanan—— [*Re-enter maidservant.*]
Have you called her?

MAIDSERVANT: Yes, but . . . she says . . .

AUNT: I am sure it's shyness, Lawyer. [*To maidservant.*] Go and
tell her I say Lawyer is here. [*To Lawyer B, as the
maidservant exits again* UC.] It is not easy for a young girl,
you know. When I met my first husband—that was, oh,
many years ago—it took me a long time to be able to look
into his face. Of course, in those days it was quite different;
but now—actually, Maanan should consider herself lucky
that she is working in your office . . .

[*Lawyer B finds all this rather embarrassing and alarming, but he
dare not interrupt without saying something impolitic, so he
listens, nods, smiles, and tries to show interest to cover up his
embarrassment. Re-enter maidservant, followed by Maanan.
Both Lawyer B and Aunt get up. The maidservant goes out
through kitchen door. Maanan is aloof.*]

AUNT: [*continues.*] Maanan, you must not keep Lawyer waiting
for so long when he comes to see you.

LAWYER B: Hullo, Maanan; I just dropped by on my way to . . .
[*Enter Hannah,* UC, *smiling pleasantly.*]

LAWYER B: Oh, Hannah, good afternoon. How are you?
[*Goes up to shake hands.*] But I had the impression . . .

AUNT: I told him James was not back from work. Maanan, why
don't you ask Lawyer to sit down? Oh, Lawyer, I must
leave you now: the children are waiting to be fed.
[*Turning to leave.*] But I hope you will be calling again.

LAWYER B: Thank you, I shall.
[*Exit Aunt* L. *There is a long pause, during which Maanan, who
is still standing aloofly at the door* UC, *looks directly at
Lawyer B, who begins to grow uncomfortable and lose some of
his confidence.*]

HANNAH: Please sit down, Lawyer. I am sure James will be
home soon.

LAWYER B: Oh, no, thank you. Actually, I only dropped by
on my way to keep an appointment—very urgent; but I
shall be back again, if you don't mind; please tell James
I'll be back—oh, I shan't be long . . .
[*Turns to leave.*] Good-bye, Hannah.

HANNAH: [*following Lawyer B to door* L.] Good-bye, Lawyer, I'll
tell James. [*Returning.*] Maanan, what's the matter with
you? Aren't you well?

MAANAN: Mother, I must tell you something.

HANNAH: Yes, Maanan, what is it?

MAANAN: I will never go to Lawyer Bonu's office again, Mother.
I intend telling Father so today when he comes home.
[*A pause.*] Can you help me, Mother?

HANNAH: Now tell me, what's all this about? I've known all
along that you don't like working in that office, but I
hadn't thought that you were finding it so hard.

MAANAN: I've never liked the idea of being a lawyer.

HANNAH: I know that.

MAANAN: And now I detest the work.

HANNAH: Yes.

MAANAN: What's more, I hate Lawyer Bonu.

HANNAH: Your father wouldn't like to hear you say that.

MAANAN: I know, Mother; Father will not listen to anything against Lawyer Bonu, but I'm afraid I must tell him just that.

HANNAH: You must be careful, Maanan.

MAANAN: Yes, Mother, I know Father's temper; but how careful can I be? I can't go back to that office again, and I think the sooner I get Father to realize that, the better for all of us.

HANNAH: Has Lawyer been giving you more work than you can do?

MAANAN: Yes, Mother, and worse than that. [*There is an embarrassing pause.*] Lawyer Bonu has been worrying me. [*A pause; then, as if she cannot control her emotions any longer.*] For more than two months now he has been worrying me. Not a moment's peace. He stands over me at my table and won't leave me alone to work. He bends over me and wants to kiss me. He follows me everywhere with his eyes.

HANNAH: This is serious.

MAANAN: It's true, Mother. I'm not imagining it. It's got to a point where I simply cannot concentrate on anything in that office. And now his two clerks are beginning to notice things.

HANNAH: That's not going to be good for your good name.

MAANAN: I know, Mother. That's why we must do something about it immediately. Only yesterday he ordered my table to be moved into his own office. He said he would like to dictate letters to me, and that he didn't like all this business of having to call me from my office every time he wanted me to look up a file.

HANNAH: I don't know what these offices look like, but it should be quite safe for you to work in his own office with the clerks next door.

MAANAN: I don't know of safety with Lawyer Bonu, Mother. I could have screamed when he tried to embrace me this afternoon.

HANNAH: Embrace you!

MAANAN: Yes, Mother. Luckily, he knocked down my chair, and the noise frightened him. He feared the clerks might get suspicious.

HANNAH: But . . . Does Mrs. Bonu know about this?

MAANAN: I don't know, Mother. But she is bound to know if Lawyer Bonu carries on like this.

HANNAH: This is hard.

MAANAN: I can't think of anything else but tell Father about it; and since I'm sure he won't tolerate such an accusation from me, I suppose I shall just have to tell him that I have made up my mind not to continue at Lawyer Bonu's office.

HANNAH: I don't see why your father should doubt your word. It's a strange father who'll think that his daughter would make up a story like this about his closest friend.

MAANAN: But, don't you see, Mother, Father has always known that I don't like being a lawyer, and he will immediately jump to the conclusion that I have fabricated this fantastic story merely to . . .

HANNAH: All the same he must feel some concern for your good name and welfare. He has always said that one of the reasons why he hates the idea of your going to a dancing school in England and coming back to dance on the stage is . . .

MAANAN: That the men will be after me! I've always known that.

HANNAH: Your father doesn't put it exactly that way. He says he doesn't want everybody to think that you are a loose girl; and, of course, all the men who will be making for you . . . I am sometimes minded to agree with him, you know, Maanan.

MAANAN: At least we can make him realize that a girl need not go on the stage to draw the men after her. As things are now, Lawyer Bonu's office holds more menace than any stage in the world!

HANNAH: I wonder if a quiet word with Mrs. Bonu will do any good.

MAANAN: That will be dropping the fufu in the sand, Mother.

HANNAH: I think I agree with you there, Maanan. Mrs. Bonu has never really liked your father's friendship with her husband. She thinks her husband is lowering himself coming here so often to drink with your father. And the way she looks at me when she sees me, because I've never been to school . . . well, I don't know what I'm going to do. [*sighs.*]

MAANAN: If Mrs. Bonu thinks she's any better than you because you have never been to school, then she's mistaken. Why, she thinks of nothing but new dresses from morning to evening, and showing off at U.A.C. buying the whole shop up with her pass-book. Any educated woman will . . .

HANNAH: I don't know of that, Maanan; and I'll not have you say rude things about anyone older than you.

MAANAN: I'm sorry, Mother. [*Another pause.*]

HANNAH: Do you think I should speak to Lawyer Bonu myself? If I speak to him quietly . . .

MAANAN: You don't seem to know Lawyer Bonu, Mother. From what I know of him, he'll deny flatly that he made any attempt to embrace me. And he could be malicious too. [*Hannah looks surprised and incredulous.*]

MAANAN: Do you know who is behind all this business of my not going on the stage? Lawyer Bonu, of course. Father doesn't like the idea: everybody knows that. But it seems that Lawyer Bonu also has been saying things to Father. And you know quite well how far his word goes with Father, at any rate where our education is concerned. He knows that I want to make dancing my career; he knows that when I talk of dancing I don't mean this kind of silly, stupid shuffling under dim lights that they call ballroom dancing; he has read some of my notes on traditional Ghanaian dances, and he is clever enough to know that what I am really interested in is dance drama, with masks and drumming and . . . [*She suddenly gives up.*] He knows all this; above all, he knows that he can make Father see how great the whole idea is, in fact, persuade Father to sponsor the whole thing. Lawyer Bonu himself has told me this, and his influence with Father is great. But will he raise a finger to help me? Rather, he goes about dropping hints that dancing is immoral, that law is the most respectable profession any father could give his daughter, and so on.

HANNAH: But I don't see what he gains doing that. If he knows that a thing is good, why should he go about saying it is bad? What does he gain?

MAANAN: A lot, Mother.

HANNAH: I don't understand.

MAANAN: Lawyer Bonu himself told me, and thought I wouldn't dare repeat it. Moreover, he knew I was almost desperate about this dancing, and he had hoped to get me by telling me what he did.

HANNAH: You don't mean that, Maanan.

MAANAN: I do, Mother. After he had got Father's mind set on this law by promising that he could, in fact, get me a suitable school in London, he came to me and told me that he could use his influence with Father to get his consent for my going on the stage, but only on one condition!

HANNAH: What condition?

MAANAN: On condition that I allow him to . . . Well, I think you can guess the rest, Mother.

HANNAH: [*after a pause*]. And what did you say to him?

MAANAN: I told him I was thinking of it. Perhaps I shouldn't

have given him any cause to hope that I would agree;
but...

HANNAH: I understand, Maanan; as things were, and knowing
what he could do, you couldn't very well have told him
off. Perhaps you did well in giving him that answer.

MAANAN: It has only made things worse, Mother. Now he
gives me not a moment's rest.

[*A pause.*]

HANNAH: Don't worry, Maanan. Perhaps it's all for the best.
I'll speak to your father as soon as he comes home. This
matter's too serious for me to sleep on. Now, you go in
and put away your things. Then you can wash and come
down to the kitchen to help me get the supper ready...
Oh, I forgot all about the rice I left on the fire; I hope it
isn't burnt! [*Exit Hannah, R. Maanan takes up the newspaper,
looks at the bold headlines on the front page, and drops it on the
table. She turns to leave the room, but stops short to listen. Enter
Hannah from the kitchen, R.*]

HANNAH: Are you still here? [*Wiping her hands on a napkin she's
holding.*] I was just in time. The rice is all right and...

MAANAN: I think Father is coming. I heard a car stop outside.

[*The sound of a car door banging is heard.*]

MAANAN: Yes, it's Father all right. Shall I stay here with you,
Mother?

HANNAH: No, Maanan; don't worry. You go in and change.
I'll speak to him myself. [*Exit Maanan, UC. Hannah stands
looking at door L rather irresolutely, like one who is worried
about her appearance. She finishes wiping her hands quickly,
takes a large handkerchief from the folds of her 'ahatar' (tied
round her middle) and wipes her face; then she returns the
handkerchief to its place, and gives a pat or two to her headkerchief
as if to assure herself that it is in place. As the heavy footsteps
sound nearer, she stands in the middle of the room, expectantly
looking at the door.*]

[*Enter James Ofosu. He is a heavily built man, strong, and healthy even in middle age. He is about fifty, and looks a determined, self-made businessman. He is the sort of man who likes his drink and clearly considers himself successful in his own way. In the company of good friends he will be hearty— even noisy. He wears a pair of dark grey flannel trousers and a pale blue, pencil-striped, open-necked shirt. He carries a brief-case, and dangles his car key on a short, heavy chromium chain with a leather tab. He acknowledges Hannah's presence with a quick glance and smile, no fuss.*]

JAMES: Hullo, Hannah. How's home?

HANNAH: All is well at home. Has the day been good? [*Takes his brief-case and puts it out of the way.*]

JAMES: Well, just the usual bother. [*He flops heavily into an arm-chair.*] These commercial firms are all alike, and they have not changed a bit in twenty years! They don't mind keeping ten of my trucks waiting outside their warehouses for hours, but when we are late one minute with the goods, then they are after my blood like a pack of dogs. I wonder why they don't keep enough trucks of their own to do their haulage for them.

HANNAH: [*who has been listening to this speech with a smile, while moving towards the dining-room door.*] You would be out of work if they did, James. [*Exit R.*]

JAMES: Tcha! [*James's eyes come to rest on the box and the newspaper lying on the table. He takes up the box, reads the label, then sets it down impatiently. Next he picks up the newspaper, looks at the bold headlines on the front page, and throws it down on the table with a sneer.*]

JAMES: Where is that boy Aaron?
    [*Re-enter Hannah, R, carrying a glass of water on a tray.*]

HANNAH: He's gone to the Post Office for the mail. [*Offering the tray to James, who picks up the glass of water.*] I'm sure he is on his way home by now.[*James gets up slowly and walks towards the street door* L. *He is speaking all the time.*]

JAMES: That boy needs some heating up. I'm sure he wouldn't do a stroke of decent work, left to himself; sit with his arms between his legs all day, and go off to paint some fool picture when he feels like it. Calls that work![*James is right at the door now. He stands for a moment in silence, holding the glass; then in a quiet, impressive voice, full of reverence.*] Here is water for you. [*He pours a little of the water on to the floor.*] It's when we get to drink that you also get to drink: make us prosper. [*Pours. James now turns and begins to walk back to the centre of the room whilst he drinks off the rest of the water.*] Ah! That's better. [*Sets the glass down on the tray which Hannah has placed on the table.*] Where's Maanan? I suppose she also has gone out?

HANNAH: She is in, James. I've sent her upstairs to brighten herself up and change.

JAMES: I like my daughter to look pretty and all that; but I think you spoil the girl, Hannah. Must she be changing her clothes and powdering her face all day?

HANNAH: [*sits down on the stool.*] I don't think I spoil her, James; you know that. And I know that secretly you are proud of your children, in spite of all the hard things you say about them. But that's not what is worrying me now. [*Pause.*] I think Maanan is very unhappy, James.

JAMES: What's wrong with her? How do you know anyway?

HANNAH: What sort of a mother do you think I am, James, if I do not know when my daughter is unhappy?

JAMES: Just as I expected! You can never ask a woman a simple question and expect a direct answer.

HANNAH: Well, I'll answer your question. I know that Maanan is unhappy because she is not her old, cheerful self. She——

JAMES: If that's an answer to my question, then I'm—— [*Throws up his arms.*]

HANNAH: She looks more miserable than I've ever known her.

JAMES: Well?

HANNAH: And I know enough to tell you that if Maanan goes on working with Lawyer Bonu, you'll regret it. She hates the idea of being a lawyer; what's more——

JAMES: That's enough, Hannah. I thought I knew what you were driving at when you started. How often must I tell that girl of mine that I disapprove of her going on the stage? A man is entitled to some obedience in his own home—from his own children. And now it seems that you, too, are beginning to doubt my good sense.

HANNAH: It's not that, James.

JAMES: What is it, then? What do you all think I am—a bloody fool?

HANNAH: I'm sure I've never said so.

JAMES: Must I be told that to the face before I know? But this is the result of being an indulgent father. I toil all day all through the year to make enough money to educate my children, to give them the best profession that any rich man's children can have, and what do they tell me? 'I don't want to be an engineer' and 'I don't care about law'—as if what I am offering them was so much cow dung! And what do they want? Dancing half naked on a bloody stage and painting a lot of foolish pictures that nobody who knows the worth of money will care to pay a penny for! That's what Maanan and that lazy brother of hers want to do. But whilst I'm alive . . .

HANNAH: You don't seem to know your own daughter, James.

JAMES: Don't I know her?

HANNAH: Maanan is more proud than you think her, and I'm sure showing off her half-naked body on a stage is the last thing she wants to do. As to her falling a prey to wicked men, well, I used to agree with you that going on the stage would be the surest way of bringing such harm upon herself; but I'm now beginning to have my doubts.

JAMES: You approve, then, of this dancing craze? I don't see how any mother who cares for the modesty of her daughter can coolly sit down there and defend such waywardness.

HANNAH: There's nothing wayward about dancing, James. Do I need to tell you that? You like to dance to 'mpintin', don't you?

JAMES: That's different.

HANNAH: What about the 'Adowa' women dancers you rush to the windows to look at when they come along the street with their songs? Do you go to look at them because they are naked?

JAMES: I don't see what this has to do with Maanan's refusal to become a lawyer, or her desire to go on the stage. Maanan is my daughter, and I have spent a lot of money on her education. You know how much it has cost us to get her through Achimota; and now do you wish me to sit down, quietly looking on while she makes a common dancing girl of herself? Maanan is educated, not an illiterate girl; and if a lot of illiterate girls and women come singing along the street and I go to the window to look at them, does that mean that my daughter should make herself like one of those illiterate women . . .?

HANNAH: [*with dignity.*] I am your wife, James, and Maanan's mother. But I am illiterate; I have never learnt to read or write.

[*There is a moment of deep silence.*]

JAMES: [*embarrassed and ashamed.*] I am really sorry, Hannah; I ought not to have spoken like that; I am ashamed. [*An awkward pause.*] But, you see, Hannah, I have discussed all this business several times over with Lawyer Bonu, and he agrees with me entirely. He is emphatic that dancing is simply not the right sort of career for a girl like Maanan.

HANNAH: Is that why he is so ready to have Maanan work at his office?

JAMES: Yes; and I don't think any friend could have been as helpful as he has been. All we are waiting for now is a letter from London to say that a place has been found for Maanan in a law school.

HANNAH: I wouldn't trust Lawyer Bonu so much if I were you, James. He has been a good friend to us for several years; but I'm now beginning to doubt that he is sincere.

JAMES: What has come over you today, Hannah? You don't trust my judgement, and you don't trust Lawyer Bonu's sincerity. Eh, what's the matter?

HANNAH: I have good reason for my doubt, James, and I wish you would listen to me for once. Lawyer Bonu could be a snake in the grass.

JAMES: You don't mean it.

HANNAH: I do, James; I mean every word of what I've said.

JAMES: How do you expect me to agree with you, Hannah? A man cannot suddenly start believing an accusation like that against a friend? What sort of man do you think I am?

HANNAH: You don't believe me, then?

JAMES: I can't believe you! Lawyer Bonu is a friend, and I am not going to have you blacken him like that. He's always been helpful, particularly with the education of the children. Kofi got a place in that College largely through his efforts; he has already got a place in Manchester University for Aaron, and he's doing all he can for Maanan. How can I doubt the sincerity of such a man? And who has been putting all these strange ideas into your head, anyway?

HANNAH: Do you know Maanan's other reasons for not wanting to go on working with Lawyer Bonu?

JAMES: [*slowly.*] Oh, so Maanan has been telling you things! [*He steps towards the door* UC.] Hey, Maanan! Maanan!

MAANAN: [*from a distance.*] Yes, Father.

JAMES: Come down here immediately.[*James paces up and down impatiently.*] I don't know what's come over that girl; I simply don't. . . . [*Enter Maanan, hesitantly. She has changed her cloth and is looking fresher and even prettier, but she is no more cheerful now than before.*]

MAANAN: Yes, Father.

JAMES: [*sternly.*] Now, Maanan, what is this you've been telling your mother about Lawyer Bonu?
[*Maanan stops dead, and stares helplessly at her mother.*]

JAMES: Come on, don't stand there staring as if you were dumb. Why is it that you don't want to continue working at Lawyer Bonu's office?

HANNAH: Don't be afraid, Maanan; speak.

MAANAN: I don't want to become a lawyer, Father.

JAMES: Yes, I know that. I've heard that story often enough not to be told it again. You want to become a dancing girl, don't you? You want to become one of those loose girls that think of nothing but dancing and night clubs, don't you?

MAANAN: Yes, Father, it is true that I want to be a dancing girl, if you choose to put it that way. I want to learn all I can about dancing, and be able to dance too. But as to dancing at night clubs, I'm sure that Lawyer Bonu could tell you, if only he would, that I have no such intention. He has read some of my notes on dancing and drama, and he knows that my plans are quite harmless. He could tell you . . .

JAMES: Tell me! Yes, now I come to think of it, Lawyer Bonu has told me quite a few things about you and your dancing— and that boy Awere who has been putting ideas into Aaron's head and has been using the poor fool as an excuse for coming into this house to see you. And your Aunt Fosuwa is not blind, either.

HANNAH: James! You are not suggesting that I have been

deliberately encouraging anything wrong between Awere and Maanan, are you? He comes here quite often; but I've never disapproved of his friendship with Aaron or Maanan, because I think there is nothing underhand about that boy.

JAMES: I've not said that you have been encouraging anything, Hannah; but I know that that boy Awere is the person behind all this stubbornness, all this talk of dancing and painting and what not. And I know that he has been meeting you secretly. Don't forget that I have friends who keep a sharp eye on you, Maanan.

MAANAN: I'm sorry I have to say this, Father; but if Lawyer Bonu has been telling you all this, then Lawyer Bonu is a liar.

JAMES: What! Do you dare to accuse my very best friend of lying?

MAANAN: Yes, Father. He is a liar.

JAMES: My God! [*Makes as if to seize Maanan, but Hannah throws herself between them.*] Stand away, Hannah; I'll not have my daughter speak to me like that. Such rudeness is intolerable.

HANNAH: Listen to me, James; I'm sure Maanan does not wish to be rude to you. But I think it is time we changed our opinion of Lawyer Bonu. Don't you realize what great strain Maanan has been living under recently? It surprises me that she hasn't broken down and given in to Lawyer Bonu's constant pestering.

JAMES: Good God!

HANNAH: Yes, James, I'm not surprised that you are shocked. For a long time now it seems Lawyer Bonu has been trying to get at Maanan, without success. Knowing Maanan's desire to make dancing her career, he had deliberately hardened you against it, in the hope that she would grow desperate and give in to him; after that, he promised to use his influence with you to give Maanan your consent,

JAMES: Incredible!

HANNAH: When he saw that Maanan was still not agreeable, he attempted to embrace her by force this afternoon, in his office.

JAMES: My God! This is a plot.

HANNAH: A plot?

JAMES: Yes, a plot to blackmail my best friend and compel me to let her have her way.

[*Enter Aaron, by door* L. *He is holding a letter, and he comes in whistling. He stops short, surprised at the scene. James sees him.*]

JAMES: Hey, Aaron, what do you know about this? Come on here, will you? [*Aaron approaches.*] Now I ask you, what do you know about this plot?

AARON: What plot, Father?

JAMES: So you know nothing about it? Now, why are you hiding that letter behind you? What's in it?

AARON: There's nothing in it, Father.

JAMES: Then why are you hiding it? Give it to me. I repeat: give it to me!

[*Aaron, noticing the menace in his father's whole attitude, quietly hands the letter over. James takes it, tears open the envelope, unfolds the letter, and reads quickly through it.*]

JAMES: I knew it was a plot! I knew it was a plot!

AARON: But, Father, I collected this letter from the box only a few minutes ago, and I've only just read it myself.

JAMES: That's precisely what I mean. The whole thing is part of a dirty plot to force my hand.

HANNAH: What plot, James? There's no plot. Can't you trust your own family?

JAMES: Trust my own family! Here is a son of mine whom I'm doing all I can to fit into a respectable profession. I'm prepared to spend any amount of money to make him into an engineer—an engineer, mind you; although I never

had half the opportunities he has, I do not grudge him
anything. But what does he say to my plans? He does not
care for them. Although we have obtained him a place in
one of the best universities, he goes sneaking off behind us
applying for admission to an art school! And now he has
a letter to say that they've reserved him a place—all this
behind my back! How can I trust such a son? How can I?
Tell me, Hannah, how can I? [*He throws the letter away.*] But
I'm not going to give in to you, in spite of your plots. You
are going to obey me and do as I ask you. If I was good
enough to choose professions for your brothers George
and Kofi, I am still good enough to choose you yours! As
for these cock-and-bull stories about Lawyer Bonu, you
can be sure that I am not going to allow myself to be
influenced by them.

[*He storms out of the room by the door* UC *and bangs the door
shut after him.*]

ACT TWO

The scene is exactly as it was at the end of Act One: James has just stormed out of the room and banged the door after him.

AARON: My word, Maanan, what's all this about? Eh, Mother, what happened? I've never known Father so angry.

HANNAH: Don't worry, Aaron, it will be all right. I've known your father in a worse temper, and he got over it in no time.

MAANAN: I don't know how I'm going to be able to face him again in this house. He is more angry with me than with you, or even Aaron. He thinks I am responsible for all this trouble, and I'm sure he'll hate me all his life for it. I didn't know that he could take such offence at the truth. [*She goes and sits down in a chair.*]

HANNAH: Mind you, Maanan, so far as he is concerned there is no truth in what you said about Lawyer Bonu, and I can understand his attitude. After all, as he himself said, one wouldn't reasonably expect a man to believe suddenly one afternoon that the friend he has trusted for several years and sought advice from in so many matters, could be secretly making passes at his daughter.

AARON: Is that what Lawyer Bonu has been up to, Maanan?

MAANAN: Yes. Oh, I'm sick of the whole affair.

HANNAH: As I've told you, you must try to forget what has happened. I know your father better than you do, and I think he will get over it. In a way, it is good that things have happened like this. He has been forced to listen, and at least we can say that he knows all there is to know. After this violent storm, he will go into his room and think quietly about everything, and who knows but some good may come of all this.

AARON: Let's hope so.

[*Enter George, swinging a tennis racquet. He is in white tennis clothes, and very easy in his manner.*]

HANNAH: Ah, George, you've come just at the right time. . . .

GEORGE: Hi, folks! [*Goes and pats Maanan on the shoulder.*] Hullo, Mother! [*Scenting trouble.*] Hey, what's eating everybody? Someone dying? Where's Father?

HANNAH: Upstairs, in his room. You can talk to him, George.

MAANAN: No, Mother; George will only make things worse.

GEORGE: That's a sister for you: George will make things worse indeed! What sort of a doctor do you think I am if I can't take care of my own father?

MAANAN: Father is not ill.

GEORGE: What is it, then?

HANNAH: One of his tempers. I think you can speak to him.

GEORGE: These outbursts aren't good for Father—I've always told him: a strain on his heart. [*Puts down his racquet and makes as if to leave the room through door* UC.]

AARON: No, Mother. I think Maanan is right: George mustn't see Father. It will ONLY MAKE THINGS WORSE!

GEORGE: [*turning sharply on Aaron.*] AND WHY, may I ask? I didn't know my reputation in this house had fallen so low.

AARON: [*warming up.*] This has nothing to do with reputation. Why can't you forget for a moment that you are a doctor?

GEORGE: And why should I? A doctor's a doctor every minute of the day, don't forget.

AARON: O.K., doctor.

GEORGE: And don't forget—I'm your elder brother.

AARON: So what?

HANNAH: [*who has been helplessly looking on.*] Aaron, you mustn't talk like that. What's come over you recently?

George is right: he is your elder brother, and you must
respect him.

AARON: Yes, Mother, but he needn't rub it in so often.

MAANAN: [*like one who has enough troubles of her own, but who yet
can't resist an opportunity to say something that has been long on
her mind.*] I agree with Aaron, Mother: George is getting
too smug and conceited these days.

GEORGE: Gee! Maanan, you too!

MAANAN: Yes, George, me too!

GEORGE: What have I done to deserve all this?

MAANAN: If you didn't go about making Father feel so swell
and important because his son was a doctor, I'm sure he
would leave us in peace.

GEORGE: Come again——

MAANAN: Yes. All this business about respectable professions
and what not—it's getting everybody down. And if you
want to know, that's why Father is angry today: it's no
worse than that, Doctor Ofosu. [*She turns away.*]

HANNAH: [*soothingly.*] I'm sorry, George; but nobody wants to
hurt you. It is simply that everybody is on edge now.

GEORGE: Are you on edge too, Mother? Then I'd better leave
here before . . .

HANNAH: Please, George, you must try to understand. I'm sure
you would if you had been here ten minutes ago.
And you yourself know what it is like when your father
loses his temper. . . .

GEORGE: All right, Mother, I understand. [*Turns round to pick up
his tennis racquet.*]

HANNAH: You aren't leaving, are you?

GEORGE: Yes, Mother; I hadn't intended staying long anyway; I
just wanted to know how everybody was. Now I know I'm
not needed, I'd better not miss my game of tennis.

HANNAH: But you will come back, won't you? On your way
back to the hospital—won't you?

GEORGE: Maybe!

HANNAH: Please do, George. Supper is nearly ready, and I'm sure my food is better than your steward boy's. [*Suddenly.*] Oh, oh, oh!

GEORGE: All right, Mother: You go and see about the food. I shall come back. [*Exit.*]

HANNAH: [*after a moment's pause, her mind still obviously on George.*] Adwoa! Adwoa!

MAIDSERVANT: [*from the kitchen.*] Yes, Ewura. [*Enter maidservant.*]

HANNAH: How is the stew?

MAIDSERVANT: It is still on the fire, simmering.

HANNAH: Go and see if it's all right. [*Turning to Aaron.*] Aaron, I must speak to you and Maanan. [*Pause.*]

AARON and MAANAN: Mother, but ...

HANNAH: I don't want any excuses, but I don't think you should speak to your elder brother as you did today. I don't like it, and I hope you will not repeat it.

MAANAN: All right, Mother. [*Exit Hannah into kitchen* R *with tray and glass. While she is away, both Maanan and Aaron look depressed and listless. After a few moments Hannah enters again.*]

HANNAH: Maanan, I have left the stew on the coal-pot and covered up the sliced kenkey. I must go up for my bath. After a while you will go and see about the stew and then lay the table for supper. [*Turning to leave the room.*] You will not forget to change the salt; you didn't change it yesterday and you know your father doesn't like the salt caked up in the cellar.

MAANAN: I'll see to it, Mother.

[*Exit Hannah* UC, *taking the brief-case away. Maanan sits down in the arm-chair, wearily, and takes up the newspaper to read. Aaron, who has been standing aimlessly around, goes up to the radio and begins to turn the dials trying to tune in. The light in the panel comes on, but there is no sound. Whilst he is still trying to*] *tune in, Maanan puts the newspaper down listlessly, then takes up the box of oil colours. She looks up quickly at Aaron.*]

MAANAN: What happened to Awere?

AARON: [*looking up from his toil with the dials.*] How do you mean?

MAANAN: He was to have returned here with you from the Post Office. His box of oil colours is still here.

AARON: Oh, that! I suppose he'll come to collect it later. It seems he's doing some night painting—I don't know why he should so desperately want to paint in the night when he has just opened a successful exhibition—but he says he simply must have them.

MAANAN: If he needs them so desperately, then why didn't he come to collect them straight away?

AARON: He was scared. You see, on our way back from the Post Office we saw Father's car parked outside, in the street, so he ... My word, that reminds me. [*He gets up quickly without switching off the silent radio.*] I must take the car into the garage and clean the carburettor. The old man ...

MAANAN: What, at this time of day?

AARON: Yes, Maanan, I dare not risk another storm with the old man tomorrow morning when he goes to take the car out to the office. He gave me definite instructions this morning to clean the thing ... [*Exit through the door L. Maanan, now a little more at ease for the brief conversation, sits relaxed, with her head thrown back.*

For about a minute the room is still and there's not the slightest movement, until the curtain at the street door L parts and a man enters briskly, but quietly. He pauses when he sees Maanan sitting in the chair, unaware of his presence. He stands undecided, then as if his mind is suddenly made up, he moves towards Maanan, quietly and intently, but at the same time without giving any impression of stealth.

Maanan suddenly swings round, then as she recognizes Lawyer B, stands up quickly and faces him. They stare at each other for a few seconds.]

LAWYER B: It's all right, Maanan. I didn't know there was anyone in here.

MAANAN: [*with sudden feeling.*] You could at least have knocked.

LAWYER B: I'm sorry, Maanan, Where's your mother?

MAANAN: She's in her bath, I think.

LAWYER B: I hope she won't be long. I should like to speak to her. You don't mind if I sit here and wait for her, do you? [*Maanan says nothing.*]

LAWYER B: [*sitting down.*] When's your father coming home? Aaron seems to have no idea, said James had gone out. There seemed to be something wrong with the car and Aaron was annoyed having to work on it in the failing light. What is it?

MAANAN: [*with effort.*] The carburettor.

LAWYER B: Oh, I see. [*An awkward pause.*] I've been advising James to buy a new car, but he wants to stick to the old thing. Who wants to stick to a four-year-old Chev. these days? [*Another awkward pause.*] I think I'll fix myself a drink. [*Looks around, spots the trolley.*] I think whisky will do. Can you bring me some iced soda, Maanan? [*Exit Maanan through door R. Lawyer B goes to the trolley, pours himself a drink of whisky, and drinks it off neat; then he pours himself another drink. Re-enter Maanan, carrying a bottle of iced soda on a tray. Lawyer B meets her across the room and tops up his whisky with soda from the bottle. As Maanan turns to go, he restrains her.*]

LAWYER B: Oh no, don't take it away, Maanan. You can leave it on the table for me. I've not finished. [*Takes a gulp from the glass. As Maanan sets the tray down, Lawyer B moves swiftly towards her, so that he is standing right over her. Maanan straightens up. Intensely.*] Maanan!

MAANAN: What do you want from me?

LAWYER B: Maanan, I want to speak with you. Since you left the office this afternoon I've been wanting to see you— that's why I came earlier this evening. I'm sorry for what I did at the office today.

MAANAN: Do you expect me to say it's all right?

LAWYER B: Won't you?

MAANAN: I won't!

LAWYER B: You are hard-hearted, Maanan. You are too hard-hearted for your looks. It's not becoming for a pretty girl to be so . . . [*Maanan turns as if to leave.*] Maanan, why do you treat me like this? I'm old enough to be your father, you know.

MAANAN: I know that too well.

LAWYER B: Come, Maanan, don't try to be rude.

MAANAN: I'm not trying to be rude.

LAWYER B: Then what's the matter with you? Don't you like me?

MAANAN: No, I don't!

LAWYER B: [*attempting to raise Maanan's head by placing one finger under her chin.*] Look into my face, Maanan.

MAANAN: [*brushing off his hand and stepping back.*] Don't touch me, please.

LAWYER B: All right, I won't touch you; but look at me.

MAANAN: I won't look at you. [*Turns her face away from him. Lawyer B appears undecided; then he tries a fresh approach.*]

LAWYER B: I think a lot about you, Maanan.

MAANAN: Oh, you do?

LAWYER B: Yes, I do. [*A pause, as if taking his bearings again.*] And all the things I could do for you. . . .

MAANAN: Please keep your thoughts to yourself.

LAWYER B: No, Maanan. I want to share my thoughts with you. Not only my thoughts, but a lot of other things. [*Pause.*] You know, there is a proverb that good things taste best

when shared. [*Silence. Then raising his voice.*] I'll give you
anything you ask, Maanan; anything you want. . . .

MAANAN: I don't want anything from you, Lawyer Bonu.

LAWYER B: You don't mean that, Maanan; you know you
don't mean that.

MAANAN: I do.

LAWYER B: Don't you want to go on the stage? Don't you want
to study dancing and be able to create your own ballet?
Don't you? You do, Maanan; I know you do, and I can
help you to achieve your ambition. I can make your father
grant your wish, I can . . .

MAANAN: I don't want your help, Lawyer Bonu. I don't want
anything from you. Aren't you ashamed to stand there and
tell me that, right under my father's roof? Why do you
pester my life like this?

LAWYER B: Because I love you, Maanan.

MAANAN: You who are old enough to be my father?

LAWYER B: Is it not possible?

MAANAN: And is that why you go telling my father lies about
myself and Awere?

LAWYER B: I'm sorry I had to, Maanan; but how could I look
on while you treat that boy so well but are so cold towards
me? How could any man in my position be expected to
bear that? He is nothing but a mere student. What has he?
What can he give you?
[*Maanan gives him a long stare full of contempt, then turns and
begins to walk away towards the dining-room door* R. *With a
swift movement Lawyer B bars her way.*]

LAWYER B: Don't go away, Maanan. Please don't go away.

MAANAN: Will you get out of my way? I have more important
things to do in the kitchen.

LAWYER B: No, Maanan, I'll not allow you to pass unless you
let me kiss you. Come . . . Don't you see that I love you? I

wouldn't do this if I didn't love you, Maanan. For a long time I have loved you secretly. I've watched you grow more beautiful every day for four years, until now I cannot resist your beauty any longer. . . .

MAANAN: I wonder you have the heart to say such things, you a married man and a respected gentleman of this town. What would Mrs. Bonu say if she saw you now and heard your words?

LAWYER B: This has nothing to do with my wife; this is strictly between you and me, Maanan. Nobody need know about it . . .

[*Maanan, in a sudden fit of anger and scorn, knocks away the glass from Lawyer B's hand, and makes a push past him. The glass is shattered as it hits the wall and the whisky is spilt over the furniture. Lawyer B recovers quickly and throws his arms round Maanan, trying to kiss her. In the struggle that ensues Maanan's hair and cloth are disarranged. But she gets her teeth on Lawyer B's bare hand, and bites him hard. Lawyer B leaps back with a yell of pain.*]

LAWYER B: You've bitten me, you've bitten my hand. [*After this shock, Lawyer B seems to make up his mind suddenly. With an intent passionate look in his face he begins to make for Maanan, slowly, almost like an animal about to spring on its prey. Maanan backs away from him . . . then she suddenly seizes a bottle from the trolley.*

MAANAN: If you touch me I shall smash your face with this bottle. [*Lawyer B does not seem to hear her. He follows her, whispering to himself: 'I shall kiss you; I must kiss you'.*] I shall hit you with this bottle . . . [*She raises the bottle.*] If you try to kiss me I shall hit you with this . . .

[*Enter James, UC. He is unbelievably calm. Maanan freezes, staring wide-eyed at her father; Lawyer B, sensing something wrong, whisks round.*]

LAWYER B: Jesus Christ in heaven!

JAMES: Take not the name of thy Lord in vain. I once had that painted on my passenger trucks. [*After a brief pause.*] You are a Christian, aren't you? [*Lawyer B is too bewildered to speak.*]

JAMES: Why did you have to do this? I trusted you.

LAWYER B: I didn't mean any harm, James.

JAMES: Didn't you? I could hear you from my room.

LAWYER B: I thought you were out.

JAMES: So you wanted to take advantage of my absence, is that it?

LAWYER B: [*under his breath.*] My God!

JAMES: You deceived me, Lawyer Bonu. You made a fool of me in front of my family. It is not easy for a man like me to accept humiliation.

LAWYER B: [*goes and sits lamely in a chair, and stares blankly in front of him.*] I am ruined!

JAMES: Now, leave my house!

LAWYER B: What are you going to do?

JAMES: That is no business of yours.

LAWYER B: You aren't going to tell anybody about this, are you?

JAMES: Don't cross-examine me, Lawyer Bonu.

LAWYER B: Please, James, remember our friendship. . . .

JAMES: You are only making me angry. For the second time: get out of my house.

LAWYER B: [*shakily getting up; then as if in a last attempt to save himself.*] I am ruined if you tell on me, James . . . How can I appease you? What will you take? Look. [*Feels in his pocket for a cheque book.*] I am prepared to give you a cheque, James; name any amount you like. . . .

JAMES: You are right, Lawyer Bonu; I like money; but I also like to work for it. My God! What do you take me for? [*Shouting.*] I warn you, you are trying my temper. YOU ARE TRYING MY TEMPER!

LAWYER B: Please, James . . .

JAMES: [*shouting.*] Do you think because I am a mere transport
owner, with no more education than what I could get from
the elementary school and from hauling goods, you can
treat me and my family like dirt?

[*Enter Hannah* UC. *She looks like one who has had to rush
through her toilet; she still retains her quiet dignity. Lawyer B
drops into a chair and remains there.*]

HANNAH: What's the matter, James? I thought I heard someone
yell out.

JAMES: Tell him, Hannah, tell that man [*pointing at Lawyer B*]
that I have enough money of my own and I don't care for
any of his! [*To Lawyer B.*] I admired you and wanted your
friendship because I thought you were educated and honest.
I thought that in your company I could hope for some
of the esteem which men of my sort rarely get. I sought
your advice on the education of my children because I
thought you were sincere and could guide me. [*On a sudden
impulse.*] Aaron! Aaron! Come here, Aaron! Yes, I would
have done anything you asked as far as my children's
education was concerned. But you made a fool of me.

[*Enter Aaron, from door* L. *He is wiping his hands on an oily
rag. He had not expected the scene that confronts him now. He
shrinks back.*] Yes, Aaron, come here; come right in here.
Look at that man. Look at him. I thought he was an honest
man; I thought I could trust him. But he is a liar, a disgrace
to his profession.

HANNAH: What has he done, James?

JAMES: Done? He's done everything you warned me of. I
couldn't believe you and Maanan, but now I have full
proof of everything Maanan said.

HANNAH: How did that happen? You were upstairs I thought.

JAMES: So I was; but I could hear him bellowing like a bull on
heat . . . and when I came down to find out what was the

matter, there he was making shameless advances to Maanan.
It was simply disgusting.

HANNAH: Didn't he know you were upstairs?

JAMES: He thought I had gone out!

AARON: I'm afraid I misled him, Father. When he asked me
outside in the garage if you were at home, I told him you
were not. I simply couldn't bear the thought of his coming
to this house after this afternoon's storm—I mean,
misunderstanding. But he said he would come in here and
wait for you.

LAWYER B: What can I say now?

JAMES: There's nothing you can say. I don't want to hear you
say anything. Get out of my house, and this time I mean it!
[*Lawyer B gets up slowly. Enter Aunt. She has been
running.*]

AUNT: James, James—you must talk to Aaron. You must talk to
him!

JAMES: Now, what's this?

AUNT: He's a bad boy. [*Pausing for breath.*] Do you know who's
waiting outside there? Do you know? I have been watching
ever since you came home, and I know what I'm talking
about.

JAMES: What have you been up to, Aaron?

AARON: Nothing that I know of, Father. I've been working on
the carburettor as you asked me—till you called me in just
now.
[*James looks at Aunt in a quandary.*]

AUNT: That's a lie!

AARON: It isn't, Father.

AUNT: If it isn't, then who is that hiding in the garage? Tell me,
who is it? [*Pause.*] I have always told you, James, that if you
don't stop that boy Awere from coming here after
Maanan, you will regret it one day. That boy is up to no
good.

HANNAH: Fosuwa, I . . .

AUNT: Don't interrupt me. That boy is up to no good, I tell you. He was here, right in here, with Aaron and Maanan this afternoon; I saw him here with my own eyes. But what did your wife say when I came to send him away? I am interfering!

JAMES: Was that boy in here, Aaron?

HANNAH: Yes, he was.

JAMES: I wasn't questioning you, Hannah. Now answer my question. Was that boy in here?

AARON: Yes, Father . . .

[*With James's last question, Lawyer B has started moving towards the door; but Aunt suddenly bars his way.*]

AUNT: Please don't leave, Lawyer, please. I know how angry you are, but please forgive Maanan; she's only a girl.

JAMES: Let him go. I don't want to see his face again.

[*Aunt, still trying to restrain Lawyer B.*]

AUNT: How can you say that, James? How can Lawyer marry Maanan if you treat him like this? Eh?

LAWYER B: Fosuwa, please let me go.

AUNT: Lawyer, don't take any notice of this, I'll make Maanan apologize. . . .

JAMES: Let that man go, Fosuwa. I don't want to see him here again, I tell you . . .

AUNT: But you always wanted him to marry Maanan, didn't you?

JAMES: Me—wanted him to marry Maanan? What crazy nonsense is this, Fosuwa?

AUNT: Why did you make Maanan go to work in his office then? Why?

[*Enter Mrs. B. She is in frock, etc., a woman no doubt well off and looked after, yet somehow not happy. Lawyer B sees her first, and he reacts so violently that the others turn and look in*] *the direction of the door. Lawyer B sinks helplessly into a chair. Silence.*]

JAMES: Well, there you are, if you want to know why I say you are crazy to think that I ever wanted Maanan to marry—that man!

AUNT: [*momentarily recovering control.*] Because he is already married? Why, a man can marry more than one? If Lawyer wants to marry Maanan, I don't see why not—he is rich enough to look after two women, isn't he?

MRS B: [*slowly comprehending the situation.*] I'm sorry to butt in like this, but the maidservant showed me in. As it is, it seems I came just at the right moment. [*Turning to Aunt.*] Am I right to assume that you are thinking of a second wife for my husband?

HANNAH: No one is thinking of a second wife for your husband, Mrs Bonu. Not James or me anyway.

AUNT: Well, I am; and now that you are here yourself I may just as well tell you that if Lawyer was satisfied with you, he wouldn't be interested in Maanan.

JAMES: So you knew all the time that he was interested in Maanan, did you?

AUNT: I had already shed virgin blood before you were born, James; and I haven't been married thrice for nothing!

MRS B: That's your own affair—however many husbands you've had; but I must make it clear that my husband will not take a second wife—least of all your niece. I am a woman, and I have a right——

AUNT: Listen to her! [*Laughing scornfully.*] A woman! Do you call yourself a woman? [*Warming up.*] Have you ever worn beads in your life? A woman . . .

JAMES: [*shouting.*] That's enough, Fosuwa; I'm not having any more of this. Maanan is my daughter, and I say she is not going to marry that man—that should settle everything.

[*Turning to Lawyer B.*] Now, for the last time, leave this
house ... [*Lawyer B gets up slowly.*]

MRS B: I always thought there was something fishy about your
constant visits to this house, your insisting on that girl
coming to work in your office; but if that clerk of yours
hadn't told me to watch out, I'm sure I never would have
believed you could be so deeply involved in ...

LAWYER B: That clerk of mine did ...?

JAMES: O.K. You can settle your differences when you get out
of this house. ... [*Exit Lawyer B and Mrs. B.*] [*To Aunt*]
You've made enough mess to last me the rest of my life,
Fosuwa. I want to be left alone with my wife and
children. [*Sinks into a chair.*]

AUNT: [*with hatred.*] This is what I get after all the years I've
served you. [*Looking with hatred at Hannah.*] Whatever it is
you've given him to eat—you only know! [*She turns and
leaves abruptly. There is a long and uncomfortable pause.*]

HANNAH: [*quietly.*] Now, what are you going to do about
Maanan?

JAMES: I don't know. She can please herself. [*Another pause,
during which the radio begins to crackle with life.*] Who left
that radio on? [*To Aaron.*] I've told you to be careful with
that radio. Go and turn it off. [*As Aaron goes to turn off the
radio, James, looking at his wrist watch, seems to change his
mind.*] All right, leave it on.

AARON: Yes, Father. [*Aaron is near the radio now. After
standing aimlessly for a while, he slinks out.*]

HANNAH: I asked you what you were going to do about
Maanan now, James.

JAMES: And I said I don't know. After what has happened, how
can a man trust his judgement any longer? [*A pause.*]
Maanan! [*Maanan barely moves.*]

HANNAH: Maanan, your father is calling you.
[*Maanan stirs, then her eyes meet her father's. They gaze at each*

other for a long time; then James, unable to stand Maanan's gaze, shifts uncomfortably.]

JAMES: I am sorry about what happened. I should have known better. But how could I? How could I?

HANNAH: It's all right, James. Will you leave us alone, Maanan?

[*Exit Maanan* UC.]

JAMES: [*getting up and going to the radio. He talks all the time he is trying to tune in.*] So this is friendship for you. Tchah! Put so much confidence in a man—a well-educated man and a lawyer to boot—and this is what he does to me. . . .

HANNAH: It would seem that going to school or college does not necessarily make a man an honest friend. But you should have known this, with all your experience.

JAMES: What experience? Experience of lorries and trucks and running a transport business, and . . .

HANNAH: Dealing with men, James. You have a lot to do with men, don't you?

JAMES: Drivers and porters and lorry mates? [*Switches off radio.*]

HANNAH: Yes, what of them? Aren't they men? You wouldn't trust them with your truck-loads of goods if they weren't honest, would you? And all those little clerks in offices all over the place, who work away preparing way-bills and receiving your large sums of money for slips of useless paper you call receipts—aren't they honest?

JAMES: Of course. But these are not the people who move the world, Hannah. If I know anything, it is that this world is moved by men in bigger positions; men who have been to college and university; men who know, and who because they know are entrusted with bigger responsibilities: trained men like your lawyers and accountants and engineers and doctors. That is why I had

so much respect for Lawyer Bonu. That's why I have
always wanted my children to become ...

HANNAH: James, may I ask you a question?

JAMES: Go ahead. Ask me any question you like.

HANNAH: Would you allow Maanan or Aaron to become a
teacher—if they wanted to?

JAMES: What are you talking about, woman! My children to
become teachers?

HANNAH: Why not? You were saying only a moment ago that
this world is ruled by men who know.

JAMES: Yes, but not by teachers.

HANNAH: I always thought that nobody could know more than
teachers.

JAMES: You don't know what you're talking. [*Raising his
voice.*] Why, I could teach any teacher more about
running a transport business than he could about how to
teach! But even that apart, who cares about teachers and
all their knowledge? Eh, who cares? I have always
maintained that the measure of a man's importance in any
community is how much that community is prepared to
pay him for his services. That is the first lesson that
anybody who wants to get on in life must learn: yes,
money, money is what matters; money is power! Money
rules the world! [*Pause, as if recollecting.*] As for teachers
and their knowledge, you can judge for yourself by
what they are paid. No fear—no child of mine will be a
teacher!

HANNAH: [*after a pause—bewildered.*] All this sounds rather
confusing to me, James. You say one thing now, and
another the next moment. But I think I know what you
really want for the children—money.

JAMES: And what's wrong with that? Where would we be if I
didn't work so hard to make money? You've always

complained about living in this house—how do you imagine I'm going to build the house you've always wanted us to have?

HANNAH: Please, James!

JAMES: I simply don't understand what's the matter with everybody today. Everybody lets me down, and——

HANNAH: Who has let you down?

JAMES: And everything I've tried to do—they now tell me—is wrong!

HANNAH: I am sure——

JAMES: You are sure I am wrong! What did I say! Educating my children is wrong; making money to support my family is wrong! Jesus Christ in Heaven!

HANNAH: You can say whatever you like, James, but please don't swear like that.

JAMES: Let me swear, woman. And I will swear by my father's coffin that if . . .

[*Enter George. James abruptly sinks into a chair.*]

HANNAH: George, you must speak to your father.

GEORGE: What's the matter? [*Turning to James.*] What's the matter, Father? [*Going up.*] Is there anything wrong with your heart?

JAMES: [*vehemently.*] There's nothing wrong with my heart!

GEORGE: [*anxiously.*] What's the matter, Mother?

HANNAH: Unless we do something about it, there will never again be any peace in this house.

GEORGE: But, Mother, you haven't told me what the matter is. I cannot diagnose, much less prescribe a cure, unless someone was ready to tell me the symptoms!

HANNAH: Everybody is unhappy—your brother Aaron is gloomy all day long, and the slightest thing makes him angry; Maanan comes home looking tired and fed up, and your father's temper grows worse every day. And its all because——

JAMES: All because I want my children to be well educated—
that's it, isn't it? All because I want the best for my
children, is that not so?

GEORGE: I don't see why that should cause any trouble,
Mother.

JAMES: There you are, Hannah! There you are! [*To George.*]
All day every day they are at me: nothing seems to please
any of them; Maanan refuses to become a lawyer—well,
I don't mind that: I understand. She can go ahead and do
her dancing and drama, if that will make her happy. But
what about Aaron? He comes along and tells me he
doesn't want to do engineering! Such impudence!

HANNAH: But why should he be forced to do something he
knows very well he doesn't want to do?

GEORGE: Father, I think mother has something there. If Aaron
seriously objects to doing engineering——

JAMES: Who talks of objection? If I was good enough to
choose you your profession, I think I'm still good enough
to choose Aaron his. And you have never told me you
regretted the choice, have you?

GEORGE: I shouldn't say so, Father. But then, I liked the
profession you chose—I had always wanted to be a
doctor, so I just went ahead and did it. If Aaron is still
determined to go on with his painting, in fact I don't see
what is wrong with it. I personally don't care about
painting, and at first I couldn't believe that he was serious;
but obviously he is serious, so——

JAMES: But my son a mere painter!

GEORGE: You said a short while ago that you wanted the best
for your children, didn't you, Father?

JAMES: Yes . . .

GEORGE: Then you couldn't do better than help them to do
what they deeply feel they have the ability or talent for.

JAMES: Even if it isn't going to bring them any money?

HANNAH: This is where I think you are wrong, James. Money isn't everything. We started life together with nothing, but you had the ability, and you worked hard at what you believed you could best do. Then money began to come in. [*Pause.*] I do not blame you for wanting your children to be important, but what makes a man important? You are important to me, and that's what matters; and I think that our affection for our children and friends and the regard we have for people because they are human beings—no matter whether they are porters or drivers' mates or teachers or lawyers—these things are the things that count. We have today seen from Lawyer Bonu's conduct——

JAMES: I don't want to hear about him.

GEORGE: What did Lawyer Bonu do, Mother?

JAMES: I said I don't want to hear about Lawyer Bonu, and I meant it, George.

GEORGE: Well . . . !

JAMES: Isn't it enough that I have said Maanan can go and do her dancing if that will make her happy?

HANNAH: Then why don't you allow Aaron to do what will make him happy?

GEORGE: [*as if musing to himself.*] And after all, there could be money in painting too, if it comes to that. Portrait painters have been known to make quite a lot of money out of their art; and even Awere—that friend of Aaron's—even he is already beginning to make money.

JAMES: And where did you get that rubbish from?

GEORGE: From the news, Father. They were announcing it in the six o'clock news headlines as I entered the house. Wait a minute—it may not be too late. [*Looking at his watch.*] I've not been here more than eight minutes. [*He dashes to*

the radio and tunes in frantically. After a brief moment, the
news reader's voice comes through clearly.] There we are.

VOICE FROM RADIO: It is estimated that it will take another
six days for the repairs to the bridge to be completed.
Already the waters of the Kakum River have subsided,
and there is no danger to persons who want to cross
the bridge on foot. However, all motor traffic to and
from Takoradi through Cape Coast will continue to use
the Ankaful by-pass until further notice. And now, to
end the news, here are the main points again: The
Conference of Cocoa Experts being held in the
University College of Ibadan has opened this morning
with an address by Dr. . . ., Ghana's representative to the
Conference. An American collector has bought one of the
paintings by a young Ghanaian painter, now on
exhibition at the Arts Centre, for two hundred and twenty
pounds. Two schoolboys took part in an excursion . . .
[*George turns off the radio with a click.*]

GEORGE: There we are: painting also can pay.

HANNAH: Well, I don't think you need anything more to
change your mind about Aaron's painting.

GEORGE: May I call Aaron?

HANNAH: Yes, George, call him—and Awere too. I think he is
still with Aaron out there.

JAMES: No, George. Don't call that boy in here.

HANNAH: But why not, James? There is nothing the matter
with congratulating a person, is there?

JAMES: [*getting up.*] I don't bear him any grudge and you can
congratulate him if you like, but, my word, it is possible
to ask too much of a man.

HANNAH: I'm not asking for anything, am I?

JAMES: Look, Hannah, you don't want me to be born anew
today, do you? I've lost a friend; I've given in to Maanan;

I'm prepared even now to give in to Aaron; but to ask
me to face that boy now—— Frankly, it will take me some
time to get used to him after all this.

HANNAH: But, James ...

JAMES: If you insist, then I must leave this room. [*He turns and
goes out. He does not bang the door. Hannah and George look
at each other.*]

GEORGE: I shall call them. [*Exit. We hear his voice backstage as he
calls to Aaron and Awere. Hannah stands like one who has
suddenly lost her confidence. Enter Aaron, Awere, and George.*]

HANNAH: Congratulations, Awere, we've heard of your good
luck.

AWERE: Thank you. We heard about it ourselves only a
moment ago on the radio in the bar across the
street.

HANNAH: Aaron, your father says you can paint. [*Aaron does
not react.*]

GEORGE: Come on, Aaron, show some pleasure.

AARON: What made him change his mind?

GEORGE: Mother's persuasion.

AARON: Nothing else?

GEORGE: And Awere's success.

AARON: How?

GEORGE: Father heard the announcement on the radio, of
course.

AARON: So! And now he thinks I can paint.

GEORGE: Why not?

AARON: Because he heard there could be money in painting?
Suppose now that I refused to paint?

AWERE: What's wrong with money, Aaron?

AARON: You know my views about that, don't you?

GEORGE: Now come, Aaron. You've been very lucky, come to think of it. And if I were you I would go out and paint like mad—and make all the money I can while Father's mood holds.

AARON: To hell with money! To hell with everybody and their talk of money. [*Turns to leave.*]

GEORGE: What's biting you, old boy?

AARON: Do you practise medicine because of the money you make out of it?

GEORGE: I love my work, of course; but I cannot shut my eyes to the fact that it does earn me a living.

AARON: Then to hell with you!

AWERE: Your mother is here, Aaron.

AARON: I'm fed up—fed up fit to burst! Why can't a chap do what he wants to do because he simply loves doing it? Why?

HANNAH: Shut up, Aaron. It's time someone talked sense into your head. Who do you think you are? Wait till you paint enough good pictures for people to want to pay anything for them, then you can tell them to go away with their money. For the present, I would thank your father if I were you, and take the opportunity he has given you. And when you feel like it, you should apologize for being so rude here a moment ago.

GEORGE: Bravo, Mother.

HANNAH: [*coolly.*] Call Maanan, George. [*George goes out through door* UC, *shouts twice for Maanan, and returns.*]

HANNAH: Before I go away to see about supper, I must congratulate you again, Awere. You have done well, and we all hope you get on as you've started. [*Enter Maanan.*] Maanan, bring Awere a glass of water. It is to give him good luck for the future. [*Exit Maanan* R.] You will not leave just yet, George. I'm sure your father will need your company at supper. [*Exit Hannah* UC. *Re-enter Maanan, with a glass of water on a tray.*]

AWERE: [*taking the water.*] Thank you very much, Maanan. And now may we each be given the strength to achieve our heart's desire in our work. [*Drinks.*]

CURTAIN